little bee books

New York, NY
Copyright © 2020 by Little Bee Books
All rights reserved, including the right of reproduction
in whole or in part in any form.

For more information about special discounts on bulk purchases,
please contact Little Bee Books at sales@littlebeebooks.com.

Library of Congress Cataloging-in-Publication Data
Names: Reed, Melody, author. | Pépin, Émilie, illustrator.
Title: The secret valentine / by Melody Reed; illustrated by Émilie Pépin.
Description: First edition. | New York, NY: Little Bee Books, [2018]
Series: The Major Eights ; [6] | Summary: The Major Eights enter a
competition at Center Stage Café, but Scarlet is distracted, both by
a mean new singer in a rival band and by an unsigned valentine.
Identifiers: LCCN 2018030541| Subjects: | CYAC: Bands (Music)—Fiction.
| Friendship—Fiction. | Valentine's Day—Fiction. | Contests—Fiction.
Classification: LCC PZ7.1.R428 Sec 2018 | DDC [Fic]—dc23
LC record available at https://lccn.loc.gov/2018030541

Printed in China RRD 0820
ISBN 978-1-4998-0762-2 (hc)
First Edition 10 9 8 7 6 5 4 3 2 1
ISBN 978-1-4998-0761-5 (pb)
First Edition 10 9 8 7 6 5 4 3 2 1
littlebeebooks.com

THE MAJOR EIGHTS

THE SECRET VALENTINE

by Melody Reed

illustrated by Émilie Pépin

little bee books

CONTENTS

CASSIE

THE MATCHMAKER
MEET YOUR MATCH THIS VALENTINE'S DAY!
Judges will pair up bands ahead of time. At the event, you only have to beat your match to win! All winners will get tickets to a surprise event.

Sweat dripped down my neck. It was freezing outside, but in here, my heavy coat made me hot.

I swung my legs as Tyson and I waited.

On the stage, Aunt Billie was talking to a man.

Her friend Kyle cleared off a table near us.

It was Saturday. Mom and Dad were working at the hospital. Aunt Billie was watching us at Center Stage Café. She sings here every week.

"Who's Aunt Billie talking to?" I asked Kyle.

He moved onto the next table. "That's Mr. Novak, the new manager."

I blinked. "She has a new boss?"

Grinning, he said, "Nope. Your aunt got a promotion. She and Mr. Novak are *co*-managers."

"What does that mean?" I asked.

"They're *both* the boss."

"Oh." No wonder Aunt Billie seemed busy lately.

Kyle jerked his head at the board. "Did you see that flier?"

Aunt Billie was still talking. I stood to read it.

At the top of the flier, it said: "The Matchmaker." Below that, I read:

THE MATCHMAKER
MEET YOUR MATCH
THIS VALENTINE'S DAY!

Judges will pair up bands ahead of time. At the event, you only have to beat your match to win! All winners will get tickets to a surprise event.

Lines for sign-ups filled the paper. Most of them were already full.

The Major Eights could perform at the café! I couldn't wait to tell Maggie, Jasmine, and Becca. We had to get to work on some new material. Valentine's Day was only one week away!

I spun around and bumped right into someone.

It was a girl. She was taller than me. Straight, brown hair fell past her shoulders. Two other girls stood behind her.

"Hey, watch it!" the girl snapped.

I blinked. "Um, sorry."

"*Excuse* me." She tapped her foot, waiting for me to move aside.

Confused, I stepped back.

"Here it is," she said to the other girls. She pointed at the flier. Taking out a pen, she wrote: "Cassie and the Cools."

"Are you guys in a band?" I asked.

"I'm Cassie." The tall girl said, tossing her hair. "These are my backup singers, Izzy and Cleo."

"So . . . you're a singer?" I asked. "Me, too!"

"Really?" She faked a yawn. "My sister Cleo and I just moved here. Our dad's the new manager of this place."

"Oh," I said. "You mean, co-manager. With my Aunt Billie."

She acted like she hadn't heard me. "In our old town, I won lots of singing awards. We're so going to *clean up* at the Matchmaker." She and Izzy high-fived.

"Well, okay. I guess our band will see you there."

As Cassie and her "Cools" left, I tugged my coat back on.

Why had Cassie been so rude?

SECRET VALENTINE

"Can you pass the pink glitter, please?" Jasmine asked.

"Of course." I handed it to her and took the purple for myself.

It was Monday morning. Even though the four Major Eights had different third-grade teachers, our classes were all together in the library today. Paper, hearts, and glitter sat on every table.

"I can't wait to see who I get!" squealed Maggie as she cut out a heart.

Mrs. Alvarez, the art teacher, had a bag near her. It held the names of all third-graders. Each kid would pick one name out of the bag. That person would be their secret valentine. Our job was to make a card for our secret valentine. On Thursday, our teachers would give out the cards for us.

Mrs. Alvarez was on the other side of the room. She'd told us all to start working on our cards.

Jasmine held hers up. "Hmm," she said. "I think it needs more glitter."

Becca frowned. "I'm not sure what to do with mine."

"Draw a heart?" suggested Maggie.

Becca nodded. "Sure, I could do that."

"Hey, guys!" A girl with pigtails skipped over to us.

"Leslie!" we said. Leslie had helped us at our last show. She'd played the keyboard after Jasmine broke her arm.

Leslie looked over at Jasmine. "Your arm looks so much better!"

Jasmine grinned. "I got the cast off last weekend."

"That's great!" said Leslie.

Across the room, a few girls waved her over and she left. "See you guys later!"

Near Leslie's friends, a girl with short, brown hair sat alone.

It was Cassie's sister!

Huh? I didn't know Cleo went to our school. So, I guess Cassie must go here, too. And maybe even Izzy.

But I didn't want to think about them right now.

Mrs. Alvarez was talking to the group next to us.

I turned to my friends. "So, what do you guys think about the Matchmaker?" I'd already filled them in on the details.

"We only have to beat one other band?" asked Becca. "We've got a pretty good chance, then, right?"

"And even if we *don't* win, it still sounds like fun!" gushed Jasmine.

"So, you guys are in?" I asked.

They all nodded.

"Great!" I said. "Let's meet tonight at the café. We can work on our cards and pick a song to perform."

Mrs. Alvarez came over. She held the bag out to Maggie. "Remember, everybody," she said. "Don't tell the person you get that they're your secret valentine. Not until after the exchange on Thursday. After that, whether or not you tell them is up to you."

"Oh, boy!" Maggie bounced up and down. She drew a name.

Jasmine picked next. Then Becca. Finally, it was my turn.

I took a deep breath and read the name on my slip to myself.

"No *way*!" I squealed.

I couldn't believe who I'd drawn!

SHE CAN SING

"The . . . Major . . . Eights!" I said as I wrote it out.

Mom had said I could use our phone number, so I added that, too.

Standing back, I grinned at the sheet on the board.

It was a quiet night at the café. No one was onstage yet. Only a few customers sat at the tables.

I raced back to the other Major Eights. "Okay, guys. We're all set for the Matchmaker!"

"Great!" said Jasmine. She glued a heart down. Paper, stickers, glue, and glitter were spread out across the table. "Now we just need to choose a song."

"How about a Silver Sporks song?" suggested Becca.

"Did you hear?" asked Maggie. "They're having a concert near us in a couple weeks!"

"No!" Becca shrieked.

Maggie nodded. "My mom said tickets cost too much, though."

Jasmine thought. "We haven't played a song we made up in a while. What about that one from a few weeks ago? You know, 'Friends will rock your world. . . .'" She bobbed her head along to every word.

I giggled. "That song would be great, Jas! We can call it 'Friends Rock.'"

"That would be perfect!" said Jasmine. She poured pink glitter on her card.

Becca wrinkled her nose. "I hope your secret valentine likes pink."

"Oh, she does." Jasmine shook the paper back and forth. Then she poured the loose glitter back into its bottle. "I got Averie Mendez. She wears pink every day."

Becca shrugged. "I got Will Greyson. We have the same guitar teacher. Cool, huh?"

I bounced in my seat. "You guys will *never guess* who I got."

"Who?" they asked.

"Leslie!" I squealed. "Isn't that great?"

"Wow, really?" asked Jasmine.

"Yep." I grabbed some red paper.

"Who did you get, Maggie?"

Maggie's face turned pink. "I . . . I don't think I should say."

The café door blew open. I shivered at the sudden gust of cool air.

Cassie, Izzy, and Cleo marched in. Cassie scanned the room.

When her eyes met mine, she curled her lip at me.

I swallowed.

"What's wrong, Scarlet?" asked Jasmine, seeing my expression change.

Maggie raised her chin. "Who's that?"

I put my chin on my hands. "Her name's Cassie," I muttered. "Her dad's the new co-manager. Her band signed up for the Matchmaker, too."

Mr. Novak waved Cassie over to the stage.

It looked like they were going to practice.

But Cleo and Izzy sat down. Only Cassie got up onstage.

The track began to play, and Cassie sang along with it.

Her high notes were perfect. She was never flat or sharp. Her voice wiggled on the long notes. (Aunt Billie says that's called vibrato.)

"Earth to Scarlet." Becca waved a hand in front of my face.

I had to admit it—Cassie was *good*.

Jasmine leaned in close. "Don't worry," she whispered. "We only have to beat one other act. What are the chances that we'll be matched against her?"

I hadn't even thought about that.

Cassie was already kind of mean to me. If we got matched against her, would it get worse?

But Jasmine was right. There were a lot of other acts signed up.

As long as we weren't matched up against Cassie's group, I'd be fine.

OUR FIRST FAN MAIL

Finally, it was Thursday, the day of the secret valentine exchange.

I waited outside my classroom. The heat in the hallway felt nice after recess.

We'd handed in our cards first thing this morning. During lunch, our teachers had placed them on students' desks.

The one I made Leslie had red stars all over it. Leslie wasn't in my class, so I wouldn't get to see her open it. I hoped she liked it.

I wondered who had drawn *my* name.

Miss Taylor, my teacher, opened the door. She smiled. "All right, class, come on in."

We hurried past her.

"Cool!" a kid shouted when she reached her desk.

"Hey, nice!" called someone else.

I rounded the corner of my row and stopped.

"Wow," I breathed.

A white paper heart sat on my desk. The edges were red lace. Purple glitter dotted the heart. But best of all, in the middle was a drawing of—us! It was the Major Eights!

Below the drawing, there was a note. The letters were pink and blue. It said:

I squealed. We'd gotten our first piece of fan mail! Flipping the card over, though, I frowned when I saw it wasn't signed.

Who had written it?

THE LIST GOES UP

MATCHMAKER'S LIST

"Here?" Jasmine asked.

I stood in front of the mic stand. "A tiny bit lower."

She lowered it more. "Now?"

"Perfect."

That night, we were onstage at the café. The staff was cleaning up for a show later on. Aunt Billie said they had an hour free and we could practice, like Cassie had the other day.

Becca plugged in her guitar. Maggie rolled her sticks on the drums.

"You guys all set?" I asked.

"Let me tune up some." Becca nodded to Jasmine, who stood behind the keyboard. Jasmine played notes for her, one at a time. Becca plucked each of the strings on her guitar until they all matched.

I couldn't wait any longer. Opening my bag, I pulled out the card. "Guys, look!" I waved it in the air. "We got fan mail!"

The rest of the group crowded around me.

"That's us!" shouted Becca. "They drew our band."

"And they wrote such nice things," said Maggie.

"But who's it from?" asked Jasmine.

I shrugged. "It wasn't signed."

"So, this is from the person who drew your name?" asked Maggie.

I nodded. "Do you guys know who had you?"

"Mine was from Kevin." Jasmine grinned at Maggie. "You know, from your science project."

"Oh, cool!" Maggie exclaimed. "Mine was from a girl in Becca's class, I think. Emma something."

"How about you, Becca?" I asked.

Becca shook her head. "I don't know. It was the best valentine ever, but no one signed it." She reached into her bag and pulled it out. "See?"

She held out a huge, black heart. It was covered in tiny silver dots. The note said:

Happy Valentine's Day to a Great Friend!

"Um . . . *black*?" Jasmine asked. "That's not a Valentine's Day color."

"But it's the best, right?" Becca grinned. "Whoever it is, they know what I like."

"Okay, but who wrote *Scarlet's*?" asked Maggie.

Jasmine bounced up and down. "I've got it! I bet it was Leslie."

I nodded. Of course! That was it.

The card had to be from Leslie. She was so nice and always ready to help out the band.

How funny! If it was true, we'd each drawn each other's names!

An hour later, we were offstage. More people had arrived, and tonight's band was setting up.

"Great job today, everyone!" Jasmine said. She lugged her keyboard to the door.

"We're going to *rock* this song, I just know it!" I said.

Becca stared at the board. "Uh, guys . . ." she called.

"The lists are up!" squealed Maggie. "Who are we matched against?"

I quickly scanned the piece of paper. Finally, I saw the Major Eights. Running my finger across the paper, I found our opponent.

My jaw dropped.

"Whoa, they're good," worried Becca.

Jasmine swallowed. "Well, it doesn't matter if we win or lose, right? Just as long as we have fun."

But I felt sick to my stomach.

We were matched with Cassie and the Cools.

CASSIE'S THREAT

The next day, I jumped whenever I got called on. In art, I spilled a cup of paint. And after that, I forgot what 6 x 8 is. (It's 48.)

I couldn't stop worrying about Cassie. Would she be even meaner to me now?

But maybe I was being silly.

Finally, the last bell rang. I was packing up when I noticed something sticking out of my backpack a little bit. Confused, I pulled it out.

It was a card!

"Hey," I said to the boy next to me. "We only had to make *one* card for our secret valentine, right?"

He nodded, hefting his bag up on his shoulders.

I opened the card. Inside, there was another drawing of the band again. I was in front, singing my heart out.

The note was written in pink and blue again. It said:

Good luck in the Matchmaker! I'll be there cheering for you tomorrow.

Wow! My secret valentine wasn't just being nice. He or she really *was* a fan!

I thought about it. Had we told Leslie about the Matchmaker?

Still staring at the card, I stepped into the hall.

Oof!

I'd bumped right into Cassie. Izzy and Cleo stood behind her.

Cassie put her hands on her hips.

I swallowed.

"I saw we're matched up against you," Cassie said, tossing her hair to the side. "Too bad for you, because when it comes to music competitions, I never lose. Isn't that right, Cleo?"

Cleo was looking down the hall. "What? Um . . . yeah."

Cassie glared at her. "A bit more help here, Cleo." Then she saw the card in my hand. Her upper lip wrinkled. "What's *that*?"

"This?" I held it up, grinning. "This is fan mail. For my band."

She snatched it away.

"Hey!" I protested.

I grabbed for it, but Cassie was too tall. She held it up, out of my reach, and opened it. "Well, it's not very good. Is this supposed to be *you*?" She pointed to the sketch.

Jumping, I took it back. "Yes. And *I* think it's great!"

Cassie yawned. "How very cute. We're going to go practice now. Not that we even need to." Then she leaned in closer. "You know, I get angry when I don't win, Scarlet," she hissed. "I wouldn't want to be you if that happens."

She, Izzy, and Cleo stalked off down the hall.

Shaking, I met the other Major Eights at the bus stop. Leslie was with them.

Maggie's eyes lit up when she saw the card in my hand. "You got *another* one?" she asked. "It's so pretty!"

"What? Oh, yeah," I muttered. I handed it to her.

"It's from you, right, Leslie?" asked Jasmine.

Leslie shook her head. "Nope. I got a boy in my class," she said. "By the way, Scarlet, thank you for my valentine!"

I smiled. "I'm glad you liked it!"

"I *loved* it!"

I glanced at where Cassie stood nearby. She was giggling with Izzy.

My smile faded.

"Are you okay, Scarlet?" asked Becca.

I shook my head. "It's Cassie. She's been teasing me since the Matchmaker list came out. Just now, she told me she gets mad when she doesn't win. She made it sound like something bad will happen if she loses tomorrow."

"That's awful, Scarlet!" Jasmine gasped.

"Why would she say that?" Leslie frowned.

I shrugged. "She's been mean to me ever since I met her at the café last week."

Becca put a hand on my arm. "We've got to tell someone."

I shuffled my feet. "I don't want to be a tattletale."

Jasmine frowned. "You're not being a tattletale. Becca's right. You've got to tell a grown-up about Cassie. Maybe your aunt? She knows Cassie and Cleo's dad."

I sighed. "Okay, I think you may be right."

Saturday morning, we pulled up to the café.

"I have errands to run," said my mom. "But your dad and I will be here before the Matchmaker starts. Aunt Billie's going to help you set up."

"*Grrr!*" growled Tyson. He held up a toy dinosaur. "T. rex and me are coming to see you, too!"

I tried to smile for my brother. "I'll see you guys later." I got out, waved, and walked to the front door.

Mom had taken out my cornrows this morning and combed my hair out. She'd put a bow on one side. Most of the time, wearing my hair natural makes me feel good. But today, it didn't help. I felt like Tyson's T. rex was jumping around in my stomach.

Inside the café, it was chaos.

Most of the tables were gone. In their place sat rows of chairs. Coats, cases, and bags were everywhere. People I'd never seen before talked and laughed as they warmed up all over the place.

"Scarlet! There you are." Aunt Billie waved me over. "I don't think the rest of the Major Eights are here yet." She checked her watch. "But it's still early. I have to go backstage for a bit. Want to come?"

I nodded and followed her.

"Are you nervous?" she asked once we were backstage. It was quiet. None of the musicians were allowed back here yet.

"Who, me? I don't *do* nervous."

But my stomach got tighter.

Aunt Billie pulled a box onto a table. She raised an eyebrow at me. "That doesn't sound like you really mean it."

I let out a deep breath. "Actually, you know Mr. Novak's kid? Cassie?"

"Of course. Gerald and I go way back. I know Cassie *and* Cleo." Aunt Billie put a hand on her hip. "You know you can tell me anything, sweetie."

I looked down at my hands. My friends would be here soon. So would Cassie.

"It's just . . . Cassie's been really mean to me. And now with our bands competing, it's gotten worse. Yesterday, she told me she always wins. She made it sound like something bad would happen if she lost today."

Aunt Billie put a hand on my arm. "Thank you for telling me. I'm so sorry she's acted this way toward you."

"Why would she say those things, Aunt Billie?"

"It sounds like she's jealous of you."

I frowned. "Jealous? Of what?"

Aunt Billie pulled some gold envelopes out of the box. Before I could ask what they were for, she said, "I don't know, Scarlet. But maybe she thinks if she can make you upset, she won't have to be jealous of you."

Hmm. I wasn't so sure about that.

"Your mom said you got some fan mail this week," said Aunt Billie. "Is that true?"

"Yeah," I said. "But I still don't know who it's from."

"It's hard to be new, you know," sighed Aunt Billie. "And it's hard to compete against a band who has fans when you don't. Wouldn't you feel jealous if you were in Cassie's shoes?"

"I don't know," I said.

"Jealous or not, Cassie shouldn't have picked on you. I'll talk to her father about it right away." She put an arm around me and winked. "But people are harder to be afraid of when you understand them."

"Thanks, Aunt Billie." I hugged her.

I was starting to feel better. And thinking about the fan mail, I started to get excited.

Even if Cassie didn't like us, other people did.

And if I could focus on our fans, I could do this.

8

PINK AND BLUE INK

Two hours later, it was time.

Cassie and the Cools stood ready to take the stage. We were up right after them. All of us waited backstage.

Cassie shot me a glare.

"Did you tell your aunt?" whispered Becca.

I nodded. "She's going to talk to Cassie's dad about it, but I don't know if it happened yet."

Cassie pointed at me. She and Izzy whispered something to each other and snickered.

"My guess would be no," muttered Maggie.

"And now, it's time for match number five," Kyle announced from the stage. "First up, let's hear it for Cassie and the Cools!"

But Cassie was so busy glaring at me that she didn't hear Kyle. Cleo stepped onstage, ahead of her. Once Cassie saw it, she pushed in front of Izzy to be next in the spotlight.

"Try not to think about her," Jasmine said. "Think about our fans, like the secret one who gave you the valentine, or even Lucy Landon."

"I wonder who wrote the valentine," said Maggie. "They said they'd be here today."

"Did you ever find out who made your card, Becca?" I asked.

Becca shook her head.

Maggie looked down and bit her lip. Then she burst out giggling. "It was me! I drew your name, Becca."

Becca laughed with Maggie. "*Of course* you'd know I like black! Thanks, Maggie!"

The two of them hugged.

Cassie's song began. We peeked around the curtain to watch.

Cassie was at a mic by herself. She was singing really well, just like before.

The T. rex was back in my stomach.

Maggie nudged me. "Hey. What's up with Izzy and Cleo?"

They were sharing another mic to the side of Cassie. One of them was singing in the wrong pitch.

"Yikes!" I breathed.

It didn't stop there.

Next, Izzy and Cleo tried to clap. But they weren't clapping at the same time.

Cassie turned to glare at them. She waved a hand at them to catch up.

As a result, they sang faster. But then Cleo stopped singing. It looked like she couldn't remember the words.

When it was over, Kyle hurried back onstage. "Thanks, girls," he said into the mic. "Cassie and the Cools, everybody." The audience clapped politely.

Cassie stomped down the stairs in a major huff. Izzy and Cleo meekly followed her.

"And next up for match number five, the Major Eights!" Kyle announced.

Jasmine, Maggie, Becca, and I took the stage as Kyle rushed off.

Cassie sat down in the first row. Right in front of my mic. She crossed her arms and smirked at me.

"C'mon, Scarlet," whispered Becca. "You've totally got this."

Maggie nodded at me.

Jasmine gave a thumbs-up.

And then something occurred to me. Cassie and the Cools hadn't done very well. And it was because they weren't a team.

We were a team. And with my friends behind me, I could do anything.

I kept my eyes off of Cassie. Instead, I tried to focus on Cleo.

She was sitting in the front, too.

She took out some paper.

Two pens were in her hand, and she was switching back and forth.

I gasped. The pens were pink and blue!

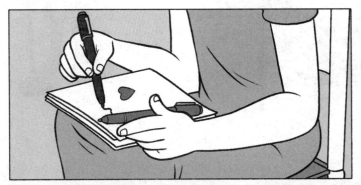

THE WINNERS

Behind me, Becca picked a few notes on the guitar. Jasmine broke up a chord on the keyboard.

I tapped my foot, counting the beats in my head. Then I sang: "It may seem like you're all alone . . . like you don't have a place to call home. . . ."

While I sang, I couldn't stop thinking about Cleo.

Was *she* our secret fan?

But she was one of Cassie's "Cools." Why would she be rooting for us?

Maggie's sticks rolled over every drumbeat in the set, finally building up to the chorus.

"Friends will rock your world . . . if you can be a team . . ."—I bobbed my head on each beat as I sang— "'Cause with a true friend, you're free to chase your dreams."

Becca went off on her guitar solo. We played the chorus one more time, quieter. Finally, Becca strummed the last chord.

The crowd went wild. *Everyone* was on their feet clapping!

Not Cassie and her Cools, though. Cassie just glared at me, hard.

Cleo stole a quick glance at her sister. Then she started clapping, too!

At the back of the room, the three judges bent their heads together in discussion.

I bit my lip as they wrote on a piece of paper. They handed it to Kyle, and he ran it up to Aunt Billie, who was onstage with us now. A sparkly gold envelope was in her hand. "Would Cassie and the Cools come back onstage, please?" she said into the mic.

Cassie, Izzy, and Cleo climbed the steps. Cassie was smiling now. The three of them stood on one side of Aunt Billie.

The Major Eights were on Aunt Billie's other side. We squeezed each other's hands.

"I have the judges' decision here," Aunt Billie said. "The winner of this matchup is . . ."

I held my breath.

Maggie and Becca squeezed my hands harder. Jasmine bounced up and down.

". . . the Major Eights!"

"YES!" I squealed loudly. We piled in for a group hug.

"Here you go, girls." Aunt Billie handed us the gold envelope. Away from the mic, she whispered to me, "I'm proud of you. Winner or not, you did a great job."

"Thanks." I grinned.

I couldn't believe it—we'd won our round of the Matchmaker!

Aunt Billie announced a short break.

Jasmine, Maggie, Becca, and I all skipped off the stage. Cassie was at the bottom of the steps.

"It's *your* fault, Cleo!" she said. "Who doesn't know how to *clap*? You totally messed me up."

Cleo frowned. "It's not my fault. All we ever did in practice was watch *you* sing!"

Cassie turned to me. "Those judges are nuts. I'm a way better singer than you."

I put my hands on my hips. "You might try being a better *friend*."

"And you can leave Scarlet alone." Jasmine folded her arms as she stood next to me. So did Becca and Maggie.

Then a crazy thing happened. Cleo stepped over and joined us! She folded her arms, too.

Cassie opened her mouth, but no words came out.

Izzy looked between Cassie and Cleo.

"Cassie," a loud voice called out.

We all looked up. It was Mr. Novak.

Cassie looked like she'd swallowed spoiled milk. "Uh . . . hi, Dad."

He came closer. "Cassie, Scarlet's aunt tells me you've been saying some very unfriendly things to Scarlet. Is that true?"

Cassie stared at the floor. She nodded.

"What do you have to say for yourself, young lady?"

"Mfsrrrry," she mumbled.

"What?" I said.

"I'm . . . sorry," she muttered.

I took a deep breath. "I forgive you." Trying to be nice, I added, "You do sing really well."

She raised her chin. "I know." She glanced at her dad. "I mean, thanks." Shuffling her feet, she added, "You guys did a good job, too."

"Thanks, Cassie. That means a lot," I said.

"Your mom's waiting to take you, Izzy, and Cleo home," Mr. Novak told Cassie sternly. "We'll talk more about this tonight. I'll walk you to the car." Mr. Novak turned to us. "And congratulations, girls."

"Thanks." I smiled. Then I tapped Cleo's arm. "Wait! You're our secret fan, right?"

Cleo's cheeks turned pink. She nodded. "We saw you perform at Tony's Tacos."

"You did?" I asked.

Cleo nodded again. "We'd just moved here. You guys were so good! But Cassie was so jealous. She just talked about how she was so much better."

Wow. Aunt Billie had been right.

"I didn't want to sing with her," Cleo said. "I just hate it when she's mad at me. I should learn to stand up to her more, though."

"Cleo." I smiled. "Your drawings were *so good*. You helped me believe in myself."

"Really?" Cleo asked.

"We *all* loved your cards," Maggie said. Becca and Jasmine nodded.

Cleo beamed. "I love art. If you ever need band posters, just let me know!"

"Thanks!" I said.

The whole band gave Cleo a hug, then she ran to catch up with her dad. "Happy Valentine's Day!" she called over her shoulder.

"You, too!" we shouted as Cleo went out the door with her dad.

"You know," said Becca, arching an eyebrow, "we still have that envelope to open."

"Let's do it!" I shouted.

The four of us each had a hand on the envelope while I reached inside.

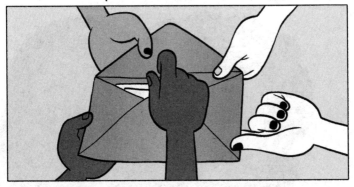

"Is this what I think it is?" squealed Jasmine.

"Oh my gosh, oh my gosh, oh my gosh!" shrieked Maggie.

I pulled them out. "The Silver Sporks concert?!" I gasped.

There were enough tickets for all of us—plus two extra!

We jumped up and down, screaming.

"Thanks for being such great friends, guys," I said.

"Of course!" exclaimed Jasmine.

"You bet," said Becca.

"Anytime," cheered Maggie.

Piling in for a group hug, we almost fell over.

We were going to see the Silver Sporks!

Read on for a sneak peek from

Tales of
SASHA
#1

The Big
Secret

by Alexa Pearl
illustrated by Paco Sordo

CHAPTER 1) Go! Go! Go!

"Sasha! Come back!"

Sasha's ears perked up, but she did not stop running. She was having too much fun. She ran past her friends. She ran past her two sisters. Faster and faster. The wind flowed through her glossy mane. The sun felt warm on her back. The spring grass was bright green beneath her hooves.

Up ahead, she spotted the stream. She did not slow down. She ran toward it.

One . . . two . . . three! Sasha counted to herself. Then she leaped into the air. Her body felt so light it was like she was floating in the clouds. *This is the best feeling EVER!* she thought.

Sasha landed on the other side of the stream. A forest of tall trees stood in front of her.

"Sasha! Come back!"

Her mom's voice stopped her. Sasha knew that tone. That tone meant her mom was upset, and Sasha knew why. The horses in their valley all had the same rule: Never go beyond the big trees.

Now she was standing in front of the big trees. She had never run this far before.

What is beyond the trees? she wondered.

No one in Verdant Valley knew. Not Mom. Not Dad. Not her teacher. Not her sisters.

I hate not knowing things, Sasha thought. *Someday I will go there. Someday I will find out.*

Sasha splashed back through the stream. She trotted to her family.

Her mom frowned. "I warned you not to run too far, Sasha," she said.

"I'm sorry," said Sasha.

Mom nuzzled her with her nose. Sasha nuzzled back. Sasha's mom never stayed angry with her.

"Was someone chasing you?" asked her sister Zara. Zara was the oldest sister in their family. Poppy was in the middle, and Sasha was the youngest.

Sasha laughed. "No. Why?"

"You were running so fast," said Zara.

"Running makes me tired and sweaty," said Poppy.

Running makes me super happy, Sasha thought.

She had once tried to tell her sisters about how great she felt when she ran. They did not understand. They liked to spend their days eating grass and talking. Sasha thought that was boring.

Zara and Poppy were so different from Sasha. They looked different too.

Zara was jet-black with a chestnut brown mane and tail. Poppy was chestnut brown with a jet-black mane and tail. Their dad called them the "flip-flop sisters." Everyone could see that they belonged together.

And then there was Sasha. She was pale gray—except for a small white patch on her back. Her tail and mane were gray too. *Borrrring!* thought Sasha.

Whenever she ran, Sasha pretended that she was shiny silver. She pretended that her mane glittered. She even pretended that rainbow sparkles exploded from her tail.

Sasha wished she looked as sparkly as she felt. She wished she could be a "flip-flop sister" too.

"I'm putting flowers in Zara's mane," said Poppy.

"Do you want flowers in yours?" asked Zara.

"Yes!" said Sasha. "We can *all* wear pretty flowers."

Poppy tucked a flower into Sasha's mane, but it fell out. Poppy put in another flower, but that one fell out too.

"Sasha!" cried Poppy. "Stay still. The flowers are falling."

I stink at staying still, thought Sasha, but she tried to be like her sisters. She tried not to move. Then her hooves did a little dance. Her body wanted to go, go, go!

Wyatt trotted over. Wyatt was Sasha's better-than-best friend. He swatted her with his tail.

"Tag! You're it!" cried Wyatt.

Sasha was off! She chased after Wyatt. All the flowers fell out, but Sasha did not care.

Wyatt was fast, but Sasha was faster!

Journey to some magical places and outer space, soar among the clouds, and find your inner superhero with these other chapter book series from **Little Bee Books!**

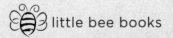
little bee books

MELODY REED is a children's book author who loves writing about strong female characters. She lives in Silicon Valley with her family.

ÉMILIE PÉPIN is an illustrator and designer who's also created children's video games. She lives in Québec.